For Cleo ~ L B

To my daughter, Banba ~ B F

LITTLE TIGER PRESS LTD,
an imprint of the Little Tiger Group
1 Coda Studios,
189 Munster Road,
London SW6 6AW
www.littletiger.co.uk

First published in Great Britain 2021
This edition published 2022

Text by Lula Bell
Text copyright © Little Tiger Press Ltd 2021
Illustrations copyright © Brian Fitzgerald 2021
Brian Fitzgerald has asserted his right to be identified as the illustrator
of this work under the Copyright, Designs and Patents Act, 1988
A CIP catalogue record for this book is available from the British Library

I DON'T WANT TO GO TO SCHOOL!

Lula Bell

Brian Fitzgerald

LITTLE TIGER

LONDON

It's my **first day** of school today.

It's **my first day**
of school today.

I don't want to go!

I don't want to go!

I can't eat my cereal.
I'm **SO** nervous.

I can't eat
my toast.
I'm SO
nervous.

What if the children don't like me?

What if the teacher doesn't like me?

My heart is beating – ba-DUM, ba-DUM!

My legs are shaking – wibble-wobble!

ARGH!
The children
look so **scary!**

ARGH!
The school
looks so **scary!**

Look at all those **sharp** teeth and claws!

I DON'T
WANT
TO GO
IN!

Maybe I'm not the only
one who's **scared.**

Maybe I'm not the only one who's scared.

I'll be **brave** if **YOU'll** be brave.

What was I so afraid of?

What was I so afraid of?

This is really
fun!

This is
really fun!

It's school again tomorrow.

It's school again tomorrow.

And we . . .

CAN'T WAIT!

Comforting stories to reassure little minds . . .

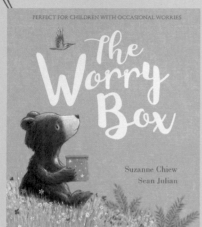

PERFECT FOR CHILDREN WITH OCCASIONAL WORRIES

the **Worry Box**

Suzanne Chiew
Sean Julian

the *perfect* **SHELTER**

Clare Helen Welsh   Åsa Gilland

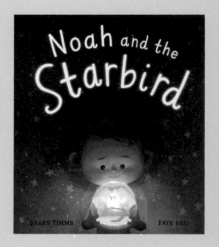

Noah and the **Starbird**

BARRY TIMMS   FAYE HSU

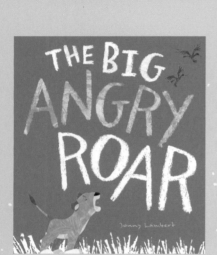

THE **BIG ANGRY ROAR**

Jonny Lambert

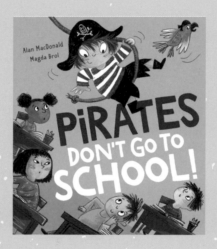

Alan MacDonald
Magda Brol

PIRATES DON'T GO TO SCHOOL!

A Little Bit Worried

Ciara Gavin   Tim Warnes

LITTLE TIGER

For information regarding any of the above titles or for our catalogue, please contact us:
Little Tiger Press Ltd, 1 Coda Studios, 189 Munster Road, London SW6 6AW   Tel: 020 7385 6333
E-mail: contact@littletiger.co.uk   www.littletiger.co.uk